VIKING
Published by the Penguin Group
Viking Penguin, a division of Penguin Books USA Inc.,
375 Hudson Street, New York, New York 10014, U.S.A.
Penguin Books Ltd, 27 Wrights Lane, London W8 5TZ, England
Penguin Books Australia Ltd, Ringwood, Victoria, Australia
Penguin Books Canada Ltd, 2801 John Street, Markham, Ontario, Canada L3R 1B4
Penguin Books (N.Z.) Ltd, 182–190 Wairau Road, Auckland 10, New Zealand

Penguin Books Ltd, Registered Offices: Harmondsworth, Middlesex, England

First published in Belgium as MARIE À VÉLO by Pastel,
an imprint of L'École des Loisirs, 1990
First American edition published in 1990
10 9 8 7 6 5 4 3 2 1
Copyright © L'École des Loisirs, 1990
Translation copyright © Viking Penguin, a division of Penguin Books USA Inc., 1990
All rights reserved

CIP data available upon request
ISBN 0-670-83461-0

Printed in Belgium
Set in Souvenir Gothic Light

LULU
ON HER BIKE

SUSANNE STRUB

VIKING

When Uncle Eddie comes,
Lulu will show him her new bike.

She will ride straight up the hill…

...then glide down with no brakes!

She
will ride
through
the
obstacle
course

without knocking anything over.

She will
pop a wheelie
without falling

and ride no hands.

She will carry
everything she needs on her bicycle.

But luckily,
Uncle Eddie isn't coming
until next year.

So Lulu has lots of time
to practice.

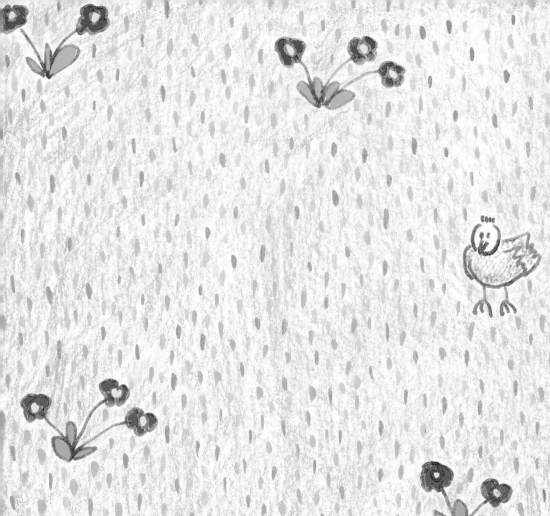